FRIENDS
OF ACPL

P9-CFX-848

HOLIDAY COLLECTION

Dick and Jane

A Christmas Story

Illustrated by Larry Ruppert

Grosset & Dunlap ✳ New York

The scanning, uploading, and distribution of this book via the Internet or via any other means without the permission of the publisher is illegal and punishable by law. Please purchase only authorized electronic editions, and do not participate in or encourage electronic piracy of copyrighted materials. Your support of the author's rights is appreciated.

Dick and Jane® is a registered trademark of Addison-Wesley Educational Publishers, Inc. Text and illustrations copyright © 2004 by Pearson Education, Inc. All rights reserved. Published by Grosset & Dunlap, a division of Penguin Young Readers Group, 345 Hudson Street, New York, New York 10014. GROSSET & DUNLAP is a trademark of Penguin Group (USA) Inc. Printed in Mexico.

Library of Congress Control Number: 2004002447

ISBN 0-448-43617-5   10 9 8 7 6 5 4 3 2 1

"Look, Jane, look," said Dick.
"Snow!"
"Look, Sally, look," said Jane.
"Snow!"

"Play!" said Sally.
"It is fun to play," said Jane.
"It is fun to play in the snow," said Dick.

Dick and Jane went outside.
Sally went outside.
Dick, Jane, and Sally played in the snow.

Dick and Jane went to the lake.
Sally went to the lake.
Dick, Jane, and Sally skated on the lake.

"I am cold," said Sally.
"I want to go inside."

Sally went inside.
Sally baked cookies with Mother.

"I am cold," said Jane.
"I want to go inside."

Jane went inside.
Jane baked cookies with Mother.

Sally went back outside.
Sally went outside to play in the snow.

"I am cold," said Dick.
"I want to go inside."

Dick went inside.
Dick baked cookies with Mother.

Jane went back outside.
Jane went outside to play in the snow.
Jane went outside to play in the snow with Sally.

"Come," said Mother.
"Come inside.
It is cold."

Jane and Sally went inside.
Puff and Spot went inside.
"Look!" said Sally.
"Cookies!"

"I baked cookies with Mother," said Sally.
"I baked cookies with Mother," said Jane.
"I baked cookies with Mother," said Dick.
"There are too many cookies!" said Mother.

Dick and Jane went outside.
Sally and Mother went outside.
Spot and Puff went outside.

"Happy holidays!" said Dick.

"Happy holidays!" said Sally.

"Happy holidays!" said Jane.

"Happy holidays!" said Mother.